LUCKY MOLLY
AND
POOR POLLY

Eve Louise Davies

There is a common misconception that free range eggs involve hens roaming outside, happy and free. Yet, the reality is that free range hens are actually kept in vast sheds with potentially thousands of other birds, few of which will ever see daylight.

Whether free range or factory farmed, male chicks are no use for egg or meat production and are killed almost immediately after hatching.

All commercial hens are sent to slaughter after around one year's egg production despite having a natural life span of seven years.

—The Vegan Society

Dedicated to the estimated 50 billion chickens killed, unnecessarily worldwide, on an annual basis.

Thirty per cent of profits from the sale of this book will be donated to Dean Farm Trust (registered charity number 1122303) Shirenewton, Wales, UK, to help support the care of very lucky hens – like Molly.

Molly and Polly were two fluffy, yellow baby chicks. They hatched from their shells in an egg factory with no mum to care for them. They cuddled up to each other for warmth and comfort.

Suddenly, Molly and Polly were thrown onto a conveyor belt. They had no idea what was happening and were very scared. As more chicks were thrown onto the moving belt, Molly got pushed off the edge.

Lots of people who worked at the factory were stomping back and forth and she thought any second, she would get trodden on. Molly ran as fast as she could, to what looked like a bright light.

The light was coming from a hole in the factory wall. She squeezed through. Molly looked around. It was so beautiful outside the factory. She saw trees and grass for the first time and the warmth of the sun made her feel so very happy.

As she wandered around in amazement, a gentle hand came down and scooped her up. It was a boy. He ran home holding Molly safe in his hands.

When he got home, he showed his dad. Dad said that they had to look after Molly as she was so tiny.

They fed her, gave her
water, cuddles and built her

a lovely chicken coop in their back garden.

Molly was so happy and grew into a beautiful, golden coloured hen. She didn't know her mum but now she had two wonderful dads, one little dad and one big dad, but every now and then, she thought about poor Polly.

Molly made a friend at her new home. Her name was Miss Rebecca Rat.

Miss Rebecca was very clever with huge, sharp, pointed teeth.

Molly told Rebecca all about poor Polly. Miss Rebecca Rat said in a very sad voice that she knew about the egg factory. She told Molly that hens are kept there until they stop laying eggs and then workers turn the hens into meat for people to eat.

Molly was horrified! Her poor, sweet, little friend. She wondered how anyone could want to eat Polly and now knew just how lucky she was to have escaped!

Miss Rebecca Rat said, "I have a plan!" She asked Molly where the hole was that she had escaped through and said she would rescue Polly!

Miss Rebecca Rat waited until it was dark and all the egg factory workers had gone home. She easily found the hole but then was faced with hundreds upon hundreds of hens, all in rows and rows of very small, tight, wire cages.

How would she find Polly?

She started at the first row
calling out Polly's name and
worked her way around

each row until a tired, weak voice said, "I'm Polly."

Rebecca immediately climbed up to the cage where the voice came from and explained Molly had sent her to the rescue. Polly clucked with joy!

Miss Rebecca Rat began gnawing away at the wire until she had made a gap big enough for Polly to squeeze through.

Polly had to jump down and Rebecca climbed down after her. Together they ran to the escape hole and all the way back to Molly. Molly and Polly cuddled once again!

The next morning. Molly's two dads came out to let Molly out of her coop.

Big dad and little dad both thought they were seeing double!

"Two hens!" little dad shouted excitedly.

They then realised that the new hen was very thin and weak unlike their beloved Molly. There really were two hens!

They decided Polly needed
feeding up so big dad got
her some food.

Little dad asked big dad if they could keep Polly.

"Of course!" big dad replied. "She is so small and needs our protection, just like Molly does!"

So, Polly was now as lucky as Molly – thanks to the very clever Miss Rebecca Rat!

The End.

LET ME EGGSPLAIN

Fluffy chicks are born
Chirping into this world,
But then the farmers choose
Between the boys and girls.

For boys have no value
No money to be made,
So sadly, they aren't wanted
Just the girls make the grade.

But that's not so happy
For the girl chicks that survive,
They have no mum or dad to love
Lonesome chirps are cried.

Stuck in tiny cages
Laying eggs, they come to steal,
Not able to spread their wings
So, humans can enjoy a meal.

Eggs may seem tasty
Harmless to the eye,
Just remember the hens –
A hard life you will find.

Keep an eye out for chickens
Baby chicks and hens,
Let's save them all and rescue them
Because farmers don't understand.

We all love our animals
Compassion we all claim,
So how can we eat an egg
That hasn't a chance or a name.

Paul V Axtell

Illustrations by Ariel Gyori.
Poem by Paul V Axtell

First Printing: 2018
Animal Tales Vegan Publishing

ISBN-9781731472311

Printed in Poland
by Amazon Fulfillment
Poland Sp. z o.o., Wrocław